We would like to thank all the teachers, doctors, therapists, and researchers who work tirelessly on a daily basis to find the answers to unlock the puzzle of the Autism Spectrum.

A special thank you to Donna, Nanny and to the best dog there ever was, Pumpkin.

-D.J. and DeDe

Pumpkin

The Therapy Dog

DeDe and D.J. French

illustrated by Jen Mundy

Hello, my name is D.J.

I am autistic.

I want to tell you about myself and about my best friend in the whole world, my dog,

Pumpkin.

When the doctor first told my Mommy about my condition, she wanted to do something that would help me join the real world.

You see, being autistic is like being trapped inside yourself.

I know that there are people around me, but I don't know how to talk to them.

The world is so bright and loud and sometimes, people scare me.

Mommy and Daddy decided that I might enjoy having a doggy, so they took me to meet a nice lady named Donna. She had lots of different dogs.

I was not scared of any of them.

Not even the

really *big black dog.*

She told Mommy that

a therapy dog would
be a good thing for me

and that she would look for one
that would fit in with my family.

You see, I also have a little brother,
but he is not like me.

He is what the doctors call
normal. Although to me,

he is not normal at all.

I am.

After a few months, the nice lady called Mommy and said that she had the perfect dog for me.

*Her name was "**Pumpkin,**"*

and she was found living on the street with her puppies.

The nice lady, Donna, took care of her and found good homes for all of her puppies.

Donna began training
Pumpkin to go to
nursing homes
and visit the people
that lived there.

My Mommy and Nanny went
to meet her first.

*They **loved** her at first sight*

and just knew

*that she would be **great** for me.*

I see Pumpkin as my best friend.

I can talk to her. She doesn't scare me. She talks back to me. She doesn't talk like normal people talk to each other. She talks to me with her heart and through her eyes.

She knows when I am scared.

She comes over to me and puts her head on my knees and looks up at me with her big brown eyes. Then I am not scared anymore.

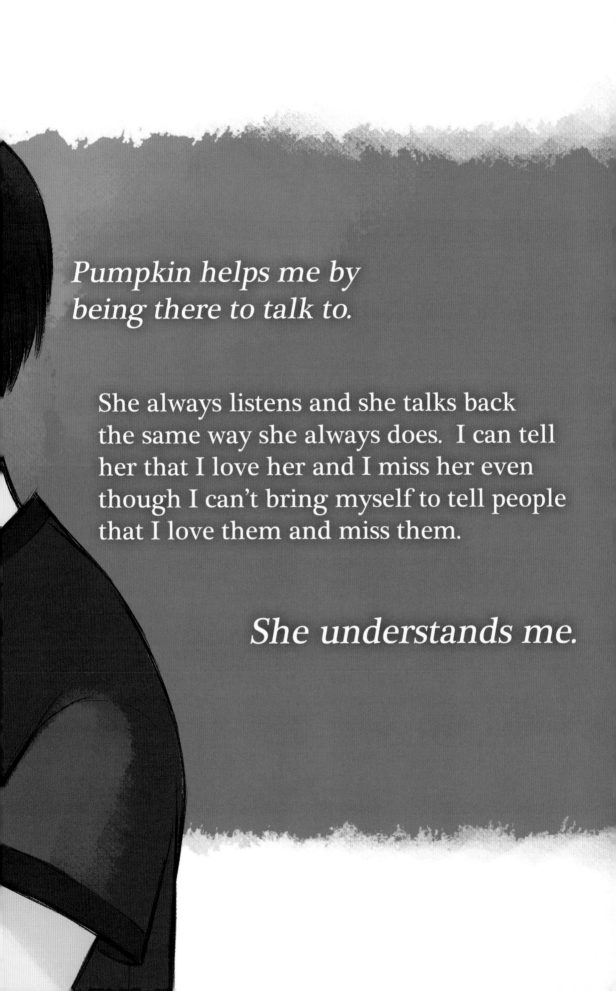

Pumpkin helps me by being there to talk to.

She always listens and she talks back the same way she always does. I can tell her that I love her and I miss her even though I can't bring myself to tell people that I love them and miss them.

She understands me.

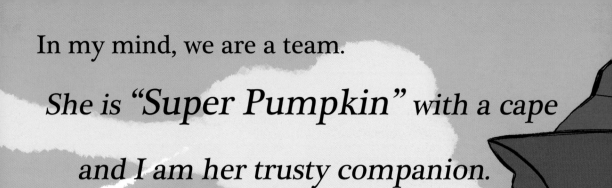

In my mind, we are a team.

She is "Super Pumpkin" with a cape

and I am her trusty companion.

We have lots of adventures together.

I take her for walks or she rides
with me in the car. She even helps
me talk to other people. Wherever
we go, people want to pet her.

She never barks or jumps on people.

They ask me about her and I can
talk to them because she is with
me. I don't get confused and I
can answer all of their questions.

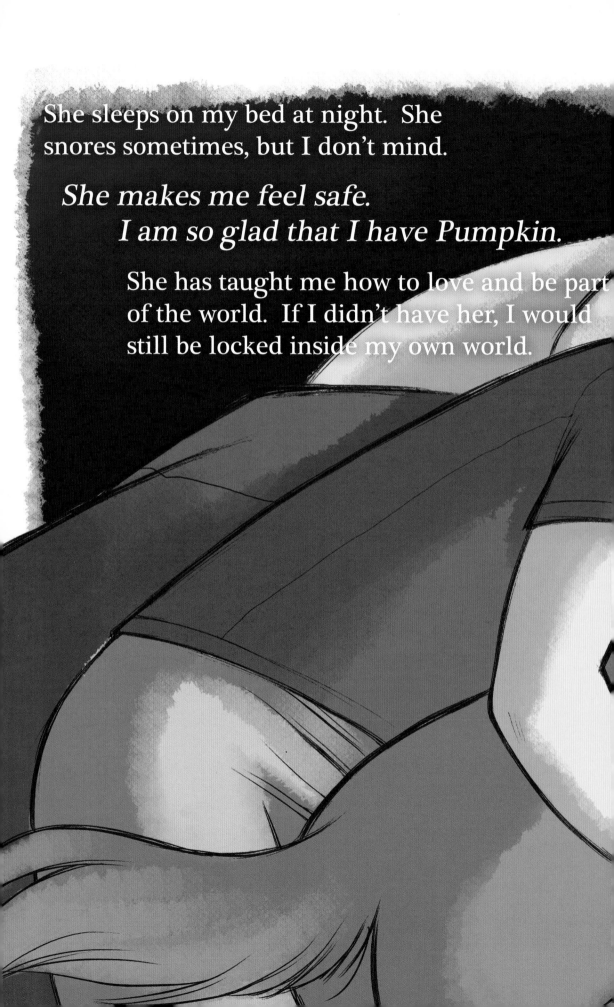

She sleeps on my bed at night. She snores sometimes, but I don't mind.

She makes me feel safe.
I am so glad that I have Pumpkin.

She has taught me how to love and be part of the world. If I didn't have her, I would still be locked inside my own world.

I love my Pumpkin.

The End

Prologue

Dear Parents,

So much has been in the news regarding Autism, but most of it is not very positive. It is such a misunderstood disorder. We wanted to write a book from my son's viewpoint. Yes, he does have thoughts, dreams, opinions, and hopes, just like everyone else. It is not easy for others to understand him. I wanted to put his plight in a children's book so that other children could learn from him. Even if he can not, or chooses not to talk to them, it doesn't mean that he doesn't want to. He just doesn't know how.

We all need to teach our children that we are all different and that it is okay to be different. That they should not tease or ignore those that are different. Just accept them for who they are and as they are. We are all special in our own way.

Thank you,
DeDe French

About the authors

DeDe French and her sons D.J. and Noah reside in Virginia. D.J. is currently in college working towards a Bachelor degree in Zoology with a minor in Biology.

About Pumpkin

This is the first night Pumpkin was home with us. She loved to sleep with D.J. from that day on until her death May 27, 2009. She will always hold a special place in our hearts.